THE RED HAT STORIES

Pauline O'Connor

The Red Hat Stories

An anthology by Pauline O'Connor

First published in 2024 by Pauline O'Connor

Edition 1

ISBN (ebk): 978-1-7396356-3-3

ISBN (pbk): 978-1-7396356-2-6

Cover by K. Powell: kpwll.work@gmail.com

For Christine,

and her fellow writing teachers.

Pauline O'Connor is a patient advocate and author of the popular *Living with...* self-help series. She also advocates for individuals who have survived brain injuries and those diagnosed with Phenylketonuria (PKU), collaborating with patient organisations and charities.

Pauline had successful careers in winemaking and education until a brain injury changed her life. Now, she is pursuing her passions for advocacy and writing. See www.PigPen.page for more information.

Also by Pauline O'Connor

Living with PKU: A low protein life with Phenylketonuria.

Living with Mild Brain Injury: The Difficulties of Diagnosis and Recovery from Post-Concussion Syndrome.

Table of Contents

The Red Hat begins 7

The Lost: Smiler 11

The Family 17

The Toil 25

The Bus 37

The Red Hat recovers 43

The Estate 47

The Gift 53

The Memory: we that are left 59

The Rush 65

The Found 73

The Red Hat retained 79

Epilogue 81

Acknowledgements 87

Kickstarter backers 89

The Red Hat begins

"Hi! Oh, you got the window seat for us. Lovely."

"You made it! Yes, it's always quiet here at this hour."

"So good to see you."

"You too, and what a great hat. Such a gorgeous red."

"Thank you, it gives me courage to leave the house now."

"Have a seat, it's table service here."

"This is a great place to have as your local."

"Plus, the coffee is divine."

"Sadly, coffee interferes with my medication these days."

"Umm, how about a hot chocolate?"

"Ooh, that would be a treat."

"Yes, you have been in the wars. You mentioned medication, does that mean…"

"They think they know what my problem is, but no one is sure. So I don't have a diagnosis yet, which is difficult."

"Are the symptoms easing at all?"

"That's the thing, I don't really know. The side effects of the meds are similar, meaning I can't tell what is me and what is the pills."

"So, the cure is keeping you inside just as much as the... Are you OK?"

"Hmm, yes. Sorry, just a bit overwhelmed. I don't tend to get out much and when I do, I feel a little lost."

"You're exactly where you need to be."

"Thank you, I just can't shake off the feeling that something is wrong."

"You don't need to be doing anything right now."

"I do worry, am I acting normally? Like we are supposed to in public?"

"Ye...es, why? What is wrong?"

"I don't like being around this many people. They might know I'm...."

"No one thinks you're any different."

"But, I am."

"OK, no one thinks you are weird. Beyond wearing a bright red hat, I mean."

"Ha, thank you."

 "Good. However, perhaps we should order before the lunchtime rush."

The Lost: Smiler

We all have a story to tell, read the poster on the station wall.

They don't want our story.

The voice in my head was becoming hard to ignore. A vigorous head shake would silence it for a while. This time, I shook too much and lost my balance, stumbling into the low bench.

A man nearby shifts. That London trick of creating distance without actually moving. An alert parent drags their kid further down the platform. Another child stares while his mum was distracted.

The voice in my head had been silenced by the shaking, so I wasn't concerned about the impression I made on the others waiting for the tube. They probably thought all stories have a happy ending. But some stories are dark. They must be locked away, hiding the monsters. Monsters like Smiler.

Monsters like us.

The voice had never returned that soon. I couldn't stop my whimper, and the mother finally noticed her child's curiosity. She looks at me, then pulls them away with the admonishment: don't stare, it's rude.

She actually meant: don't get involved. At that moment, when our eyes met, her face held that look which people have for me these days. Sometimes there is pity, sometimes fear, but there is always avoidance.

And they should avoid us, shouldn't they?

I couldn't shake my head this time.

We did it, it was us.

Yes, it was me. Smiler only witnessed what had happened that night, but I was the one who did it. The others on the street had told me to avoid Smiler. But he saw what had happened, and didn't go to the police. Instead, he'd helped me get away, unseen. Smiler has been good to me, protecting me.

Using us.

The voice hates that I did this now, work the trains for Smiler's money. He helped me though, so I must help him.

No one can help us.

More people shuffle onto the platform and I move away from the busy entrance. There aren't many passengers waiting for the tube after rush hour, but enough to keep me occupied. The need to keep tabs on possible threats and escape routes provided a distraction. Almost enough to stop remembering. Almost.

Focus. That happened, it's done. Where is the threat?

I hate it when the voice is right. Scanning the platform, I see the old lady with the shopping bag. Others might dismiss her as harmless, but I know better. Her bag was mostly empty, with a small weight at the bottom. Could be a pint of milk.

Could be a semi-automatic.

Time to move away from her. The curve of the platform would cut down the old lady's line of sight. My movement caught the attention of another passenger, a woman in a dark winter coat. She holds a red hat at her side. The person with her was new to the city. The wide stare of someone straight off a plane was clear to anyone with a bit of street knowledge. And you don't survive a tour without a bit of intelligence.

And all our 'intelligence' brought us here, did it?

I bite back a retort.

*Yeah, right. We are only mad if we reply to ourselves. Keep
believing that.*

I was watching the old lady when I realised the woman with the hat wasn't listening to her friend. She is still looking at me.

We dismissed her too quickly. Our instincts are slipping.

I checked her over more closely this time. Coat open, jeans, and knitted jumper. Her hat & phone are in her hands, and there is a bag on her back.

That's a mistake, we could disable her before she got any-
thing out.

She might have a concealed holster, but with both hands full she has no hope of a surprise shot. The woman is aware of my scrutiny, and her stare is blatant now. There is no threat on her face, rather, something I haven't seen in a long time. Is that compassion?

Don't be stupid, who'd care about us? She's just rude. Time
to warn her off.

I twist my face into the horrible grimace I had practised in reflected windows. All those nights trying to stay awake, to live, had some uses. It doesn't work, she is still looking.

What does she hope to see?

I look into the curved mirror at the end of the platform. It shows a man in an oversized green jacket, faded jeans, and scuffed sneakers. A face, once handsome, now shattered and twisted.

Handsome? Yeah, right.

I was a looker once, maybe. Back when I'd just signed up and had everything to look forward to. Back when I didn't know what the stories were really like, or what I was capable of.

But we know now, don't we?

That face in the mirror had once looked out at the world with hope. But is now jaded and lost. It looks like someone who doesn't want to remember. And why should I remember? Perhaps I've seen too much anger, too much pain.

Perhaps we've caused too much of it.

The woman had looked away, but her face was still kind. Does she want to help me?

No one can help us. We've only got each other.

The train arrives, and it is time to work for Smiler. I wait, then board just before the doors closed. As the train stutters into motion, I start on my captive audience. The usual spiel about needing a few quid to get into the hostel.

It is working on the newcomer, her initial shock turns into a reach for her purse. Her friend with the hat intervenes, pontificating at volume that homeless shelters don't charge. Any kindness in her face is gone.

My humiliation roars into anger. I want to shout at her, shout at all of them. To tell them that I didn't want to be this. That I'd fought for my country.

But we killed in Southwark.

I snap my mouth shut without a sound, and move on. What could I say that would change things? I wanted to tell her that this money isn't for drugs. Of course, she wouldn't believe that.

She doesn't know what it is like on the street. How we must fight to survive. How I was caught off guard that horrible night and, in my panic, punched out. How his arms had flailed as he fought for balance. How his face had changed as he plummeted over the edge. How his blood had been the colour of her hat. How I vomited bile because there had been nothing in my stomach. How I had turned to find that Smiler had seen it all. How vicious his smile had been. She didn't know any of that.

But Smiler knows. We've got to keep him sweet so that no one else finds out.

And that means getting his money. And that means swallowing the bitter remnants of my pride, again.

It's OK, we don't need anyone else.

I sigh, "I hate it when you're right."

The Family

Leena looked at her watch, then clutched the bags closer. Would the bus ever come? She resisted the urge to go to the timetable again, and tried to look calm. Calm, Leena thought. How can anyone be calm doing what she was about to do?

Leena's hands clenched tighter as she recalled snatches of the fraught day. Her younger sister had cried loudly. Her mother's tears had rolled silently down her cheeks. But it was her father's face which remained most vivid in her memory.

First, he had paced the living room carpet, his face twisted with rage. His hands had jabbed the air with each outburst. "We moved to this country to give you all a chance. We left our family behind to give you things we could only dream about. Back there, we wouldn't have a house like this. You live in these four walls, you'll do as I say."

As his anger cooled, he had turned to anxious bargaining. "Why won't you do this for the family? Think of what we have done for you. It wasn't always this good. I worked seventy-hour weeks to set us up here, to give you those clothes. Your mother saved every penny and went without to feed you. All this we did for you and in return, you refuse to do anything for us!"

Finally, he'd resorted to a desperate pleading. "This match means we'd have enough to get your cousins over here. They could go to school rather than having to work all day. How can you deny them that?"

Leena shivered as she remembered this last one. It still gave her a horrible feeling, like snakes twisting in her belly. Was her father right? Was this marriage a small price to pay to get her cousins into a proper house?

Her phone rang, dragging Leena out of her thoughts and back to the present. She fumbled in her bag for the ringing phone, then stared at the screen. Vik. Her brother's smiling photo implored her to answer.

No, Leena shook herself out of that thought. No, it wasn't a small price. It was her entire life. Dihaan, though he might be rich, was such an old man. Nearly thirty! Leena's determination sprang back, and she rejected the call.

Rebellion. Leena felt exhilarated, and terrified. How could she manage this? All her life, family had encircled her. Confining, yes, but supportive too. How would she manage on her own? She needed help. Someone to be her guide, friend, and confidant. Most of all, just someone to tell Leena that she was right. That it was her life to do with as she will.

Leena's phone rang out, and her hands shook as she rejected her brother's call again. Perhaps the word hadn't spread yet. Perhaps her parents were trying to keep this in the immediate family. To hide the shame of her defiance.

Another ring, but it was not her phone. A woman waiting for the bus fumbled in her bag. Relieved, Leena watched the woman laugh into her phone. Young, but still older than Leena. The bright ruby hat she wore spoke of someone happy to be seen in the world.

I need that confidence, Leena thought. She listened as the woman agreed to meet someone for cocktails. Cocktails! Not a chain restaurant where the family can eat cheaply. Leena longed to meet someone for cocktails one day. She wanted to call out, "Take me with you. Take me away to your life of cocktails, and friends, and loud hats."

Leena could do it, just step into this woman's life. They could share their stories and defy the world by making friends. They could live together in a flat, and Leena would get a proper office job. And in the evenings they could meet for cocktails and shopping. They could be best friends, almost sisters. The big sister Leena had always wanted, someone to show her how the world works.

"Leena," a familiar voice broke into her daydream. "Leena!"

Father has found me! Leena spun around, but was relieved to see her brother running from his car, which was recklessly parked across the pavement. Vik's face changed when he saw the hurriedly packed suitcases beside her. "Oh, Leena" his voice was sad and fearful.

Vik took her hand and guided them to a bench nearby before speaking again. "How could you do this to our family? If you ran now, that would be it. They would never forgive you, you'd be on your own. We could never see you again, I could never..." Vik broke off.

"So you want to control me too!"

Leena hadn't believed he could want this marriage for her. Vik had always looked after her, letting her join his gang when they were kids, and picking her up when she fell. Her brother sighed, blinking back tears as he sat beside her.

"Leena, I know you are scared, and it isn't fair. But...well, you're old enough now to know that life isn't fair. It's hard and, sometimes, we have to compromise."

"Compromise! Dihaan is a compromise?"

"Yes! Would you really prefer Samir? He's young and pretty, but he uses it, Leena. He promised Jessa he loved her, would take her to his family if only she'd..."

Vik stopped, sighing. "Well, I can't tell you what Samir boasted of. If anyone ever spoke of you like that..."

"Those rumours aren't true, Vik. They're lies, just lies."

"It doesn't matter what they are, Leena. With what Samir has said, Jessa will never make a good match now. Her family is shamed by his words alone. You know this."

Leena did know. Every woman knew what those rumours would mean.

"Samir has ruined Jessa's life, yet you want to be with him still? This isn't like you."

"No!" Leena protested. "He'd not have said that if it wasn't true. Samir wouldn't. They broke up because she turned on him, started shouting and screaming. It was all Jessa's fault."

"Who told you that?"

Leena was silent.

"Samir did, didn't he?"

Vik turned and grasped Leena's hand. "Listen, please. Samir promised Jessa a future together, and she believed him enough to… Well, why do you think her family are flying back to their village in summer? It's the only way for her now."

Leena pulled away, retreating from his words and from her creeping doubt. Samir had vowed many things but how often had Leena needed to stop his caresses, holding him away however much she enjoyed them. Should she need to remind him of her honour that often? Again and again after each broken barrier?

"Leena." Vik held out his hand, but she recoiled. "Lee…".

His phone interrupted. Vik glanced at the number, then back to her. His face was grave as he whispered, "It's Father."

Leena gaped at him. Vik only stared back as his phone rang again, and again. The others waiting at the bus stop murmured and cast glances their way. Still, Vik waited in silence, watching Leena. Waiting for her decision. Everyone was watching Leena. But still no decision came. It's too much, she thought. I need help!

Leena looked for her ally. The woman in the red hat was also watching. Their eyes met and Leena sent a silent plea: Help me, take me with you.

A bus arrived, and the woman climbed on. Leena watched her secret hope settle in a seat without another glance. The woman was leaving her. Leena was alone. Utterly alone.

Vik's hand took her own. Looking down, Leena saw the scar from their childhood games in the wild space at the end of the road. Leena had become stuck in the old wire fence and Vik had ripped his hand while helping her out.

The blood had dripped on her clothes, and Vik had been punished for the expense. But he had never told anyone it was her fault, even in the face of her parent's anger. That was the brother Leena would be leaving behind.

Their aunt had secured an emergency appointment for Vik. The uncles had gone to the wild space and removed all the wire and rubbish. The place became their playground. That was their family. Could Leena really walk away from all of them?

The lady in the red hat was gone Leena turned to Vik and nodded. "For the family."

Vik squeezed her hand, "With us, Leena. With the family."

The Toil

"That's right mate, it's the manager who ain't fit for purpose. Got the best players money can buy and don't know how to use 'em!"

The man jabbed the air with his broom, and a passerby took a wide arc around the pair of road sweepers. Charles had also been alarmed by his companion's behaviour when they'd set out that morning. The man was listening to talk radio, and had spent the hours arguing along with the conversation.

A man setting the world to rights while collecting rubbish was a farcical spectacle, but Charles was not amused. He had ignored the frustrating habit earlier in the morning, when the fear of being recognised in this council-issued hi-vis had overwhelmed him. Now, a few hours and numerous bags of street rubbish later, that anxiety had worn away on the grindstone of tedium. All he felt now was a growing irritation with the other man.

Charles kept up an inner monologue, as he worked down the pavement. This is such a waste of my expertise. It might be the best way for others to serve the community. My time is better used elsewhere.

He had been preparing this explanation in advance, re-fining his explanation until no reasonable man could possibly disagree. That morning, Charles had been shocked when the shift manager had done just that.

"Same rules for everyone," the supervisor had sneered before Charles had even finished talking. "If you don't like it, don't break the rules."

Despite the interruption, Charles had rallied. This is just a negotiation, he had told himself. This is what I do. First step, get him on my side.

"Of course, same rules for everyone. And we are all the same here, aren't we chaps?" Charles hoped his cheerful tone hadn't sounded false. The supervisor had ex-changed an odd look with the third man, the one now alongside him and gesticulating with a broom.

The supervisor had not relented. "Here, get these on." He had thrust orange vests into their hands, "then you'll be just the same."

"Peas in a pod," the other man had chirped.

The two men had sniggered, which Charles had ignored. "And what is it you'd like us peas to be getting on with?"

"Street sweeping, there are your trolleys. When the bags are full, leave 'em by the side and we'll collect this after-noon."

Charles had looked at the gutters stretching away to the bottom of the hill and exclaimed, "you mean the whole street?"

"No, this plus all the streets between Main, School, and Mill roads. But don't worry, you've got six hours to do it in."

Six hours of this, once a week for two months. It was no less a shock today than when he had first heard the ruling in court. Charles had explained that the business needed him, and that the town needed his business. Yet, the court had ruled this was the best way for him to spend his time.

In the intervening weeks, Charles had been sure he would be reprieved. It was terrible timing for his first day. Tomorrow was the investors' lunch at Le Grand Navet, with the chance to land the new development contract. The new opportunity would bring many benefits to the town. It would provide money and jobs in the community. Well, not many jobs, and certainly not for the likes of the man alongside him. Unless annoying cleaners were needed.

Anyone could see that Charles' time was better spent elsewhere. He just needed the sullen supervisor to see that, too. When would he get another chance to convince the man? Charles checked his wrist on impulse. Damn! He'd taken off his watch, judging it too flashy for such work. Now he was timeless and aimless. Drifting from one piece of refuse to the next.

Charles swept, and the monotony sent his thoughts back to that evening last autumn. He remembered the fear he'd felt when the car had slipped on the corner. The helplessness when his frantic turns of the steering wheel had no effect on the skid. The memory of the noise and force when the car slammed to a stop still woke him at night. As did the question: why had he not got out to check the car and damage then?

The police didn't seem sympathetic when he'd explained that it was dark and he'd just had a shock. They'd also been unmoved by Charles's assurances that he'd meant to go to the station to report the accident, and to pay for any damage.

Instead, the officers had come knocking early the following morning, when Charles's head was still fuzzy and trying to catch up. He couldn't believe there had been that much damage. It was just a bus shelter which nobody used.

The expensive lawyer later told Charles that the real problem was the alcohol. It was simply bad luck that George had convinced Charles to stay for another bottle of that excellent Shiraz at lunch.

The police emphasised the luncheon bottles, and stated that they would have breathalysed Charles if he hadn't 'fled the scene'. Such hyperbole. He had driven home carefully, despite the bumper dragging on the road.

And, while it had been an extended lunch, was it really the three hours reported in court? Charles didn't think so. Nor did he think enough emphasis had been given to the hours he had spent at the office in the afternoon, before driving home.

His lawyer had advised against arguing, and to impress the court with his contrition. In the end, Charles had resolved to pay the fine immediately, and to keep the whole affair as quiet as possible.

The news of a likely driving ban had been a blow. Charles had needed a stiff drink to digest that information. He told his colleagues of a need to exercise, ensuring that only his wife knew the real reason he wasn't behind the wheel any more. Rebecca was livid, but agreed that walking to work would be better for him. Plus, it meant that she could have the repaired Jag.

It also made sense to sell the old Volvo now that the children were safely off to university. Charles had endured several icy dinners before finding a suitable apology. He suggested that the proceeds from the sale of the Volvo should fund a second holiday, "Just for you, love."

A shrewd look told him that Rebecca knew it was a bribe. She arched her eyebrow, "Don't be that stupid again, Charles".

With that, the matter was resolved and a warmer home secured. Rebecca had still taken the holiday, which meant she'd been away during his court appearance.

The court proceedings had begun well, Charles had maintained his face in a carefully practised balance between contrite and polite. The three magistrates had listened with blank faces to the explanations of his business requirements.

Charles assumed he had succeeded when the magistrates had announced a smaller fine than anticipated. Then they added sixty hours of community service. A polite request to remove the hours and increase the fine had been met with, "we feel this to be a more redemptive way to pay back to our community."

At a nudge from the lawyer, Charles had retreated. Now, that lawyer was enjoying an extortionate fee while Charles swept leaves from the streets. Charles hefted his newly-filled shovel with extra vigour. The load of leaves and litter shook free and caught in a gust of wind.

The swirl billowed around a woman walking past. She stopped dead with a cry, and flapped about while the leaves slowly settled. "Bloody hell," exclaimed Charles. "I'd just finished that patch."

The woman removed her red hat and glared at him: "Don't worry, I'm fine."

Charles bristled at the harsh tone as his companion abandoned the latest radio argument to help the lady. "Sorry about my mate here, just an accident. No harm meant. Accidents happen."

The woman peeled a sodden leaf from her hat, leaving a black smudge on its red material. "Yes, of course acci-

dents happen." she said. "But we can at least acknow-
ledge our mistakes."

Charles rolled his eyes at the haughty manner, something
not lost on either of the pair. "Well, really" the woman
exclaimed. "You throw rubbish over someone and can't
even apologise. It's obvious how you got where you are.
At least your friend here still has manners."

Charles gaped at the outburst and then, to his disbelief,
the other man joined in. "I'm sorry, love. There's no ac-
counting for some people. And to clarify, he's not really
me mate, just the grumpy bastard I've been forced to
spend the day with."

"Oh, you poor thing, to be lumbered with this
company." Charles felt his face grow warm with shame,
while the woman continued. "Do you have much
longer?"

"Not long and besides, I earned this didn't I?"

The pair turned away, the woman placated by the man's
simple kindness. The opportunity to apologise disappeared, and Charles was left humiliated.

The woman moved on, and his companion returned to
the work without a word, the radio now abandoned.
They worked in silence for a few minutes, an expectation
hanging in the air. Charles needed to offer thanks, and
they both knew it. The swish of the man's patient sweeping cut furrows in the remnants of Charles's pride. The

longer he waited, the harder it would be. At last, he said: "Thank you."

No reaction, the man swept on. Charles tried again, louder this time. "Thank you for helping and for apologising. I'm..."

"Look," the man interrupted. "I apologised to her, 'cause it wasn't her fault. I didn't do it as a favour to you. But I will do you a favour now and tell you that you ain't getting out of this. The only way out of the service is to do the service. Which means you're going to be spending a lot of time doing this kind of thing, and there are only two ways to deal with it. You can spend the day being a total arsehole to everyone, making the whole experience a misery. Or you can accept that you did what you did, that it brought you here, and just make the best of it. That's my favour to you. Take it or leave it."

Another silence fell, punctuated by the sweeping of brooms and scraping of shovels. When the man's trolley bag was full, Charles came over to help him wrestle it out of the broken frame. The man eyed him up, then accepted with a curt nod. Together, they closed the bag's ties and hefted it out of the trolley. As the man dropped the sack in the gutter, Charles said, "I'm sorry, that was appalling behaviour."

Another curt nod and they bent to the pavements once more. After a few sweeps, Charles asked, "You've been doing this for a while, then?"

"Two months, got one more day after this shift. This gig ain't so bad. I was on the chain gang bus first time out. Done my best to avoid it since."

"Chain gang bus?"

"You don't want to know. Just know that sweeping up other people's rubbish is much better."

"I got two months too, this is day one."

"Yeah, no kidding. You got that first day rage. Everyone is like that. Still thinking about the court day, and trying to believe they didn't deserve this."

The man grinned at Charles' astonishment. "Ain't no mind reader, but I was just like you first day out. All anger and hating the world, convinced the rozzers had fiddled with the blower."

"Rozzers?"

"You know, the Sweeney."

"Ah, yes. What changed?"

The man paused, then sighed. "There's this family on my estate. Parents are still young, lovely folk. They got two kids, a boy & girl. You know, perfect family. Anyway, just after I'd started this, the dad was picking up from the takeaway across the street. Car ran the red light and smacked right into him. Drunk driver. Broken legs, face messed up bad from hitting the windscreen. Lost his job cause he couldn't work."

"My god!"

'Yeah, it took a while for the kids to get used to their Dad's new face, and they're still scared to go out. Scared of their own street, the poor things. The driver was all apologetic, once he'd sobered up. Didn't fight it or put the family through a court case, so the court went lenient on the sentence. Small mercies, I guess. But I see that family every day, watch them struggle along without his pay. Try to help, but...it's like they're all doing time along with the driver. Guess I figured I was lucky to be stopped before I did something like that. And, well, picking up rubbish ain't so bad. "

"Small mercies indeed, Charles," said George the next day as Le Grand Navet's head sommelier was re-filling the investors' wine glasses. "What luck that the weather has come right just as you've 'decided' to amble about more."

Henry's tipsy chortle and Edward's blank face told Charles that the investors knew exactly why he had walked to the restaurant. He'd been slightly winded while apologising for his tardiness. To Charles's surprise, the second bottle had already been uncorked. In reply to George, he muttered, "Yes, well. There are swings and roundabouts in life."

"Ah, it was on a roundabout, was it?" Henry's dig was far less subtle, but he & George chortled again.

Charles should have felt more embarrassed, but George's jibe reminded him of yesterday's conversation. Charles squashed his anger and kept his voice mild: "Sometimes we all need a wakeup call."

Henry's wine glass stopped halfway to his mouth, and Charles followed with: "Really, the outcome could have been much worse."

Before Henry could decide whether he should be insulted, Edward cleared his throat loudly, "To business, gentleman."

A week later, when Charles was next offered an orange vest, he accepted it from the surprised supervisor with thanks. Charles shrugged it on, and placed his headphones over his ears:

"Audiobook: Business Talk, How to succeed in every negotiation. Chapter one: Listening..."

The Bus

"Please move down inside the bus."

No one moved. When the recorded voice spoke again, a few people in the aisle sighed and shuffled along. I moved hopefully toward the seats at the back, but they were filled before I could get there.

I turned and found a way to brace myself. The person behind me did the same. Something firm pressed into my rear. I didn't like to think what. Any sense of personal space evaporated at rush hour. A few more passengers joined our crush before the door slammed, and the bus shuddered onward.

I longed to put my music back on, but it had already drained the last of my phone's battery. I sighed, and tried to ignore the public part of the transport system.

Coughs and sneezes vied with each other for attention among snatches of quiet phone calls. Drizzle smeared against the windows, all I could see was the lights of crawling traffic. The bus ground on towards the next stop.

An outburst of laughter from a group of young women was drowned out by the doors creaking open. After a moment, there was another request to squeeze down the aisle. Space that had been jealously guarded one stop before was now rescinded. The object pressing into me shifted, and then was gone. I realised with relief that it had been a bag.

A few travellers were rescued from the rain into the bus's fetid air. The windows fogged completely, and the space took on the cold humidity unique to buses on a wet autumn night. The crush intensified and a sullen silence fell.

At the next stop, only the rear door opened as the driver finally judged the crush too great to allow more passengers onboard. The open door let a welcome breeze in, but no one got off. Those queuing at the bus stop stepped back in disappointment. The bus stuttered onwards. My view forward was now blocked by a woman in a red hat.

"How old are you?"

I couldn't find the speaker at first, then saw the wearer of the red hat watching a man crammed in near the door. He was looking at one of the young women, who had been cut off from her group in the crush. I saw her school blazer and realised she was still a teenager.

She looked at her hands, then over at her friends. But they were too far away to hear. The girl looked at the emergency signs and then back at the man. Bastard, I thought. What a thing to ask a girl.

I saw a few people looking away, not wanting to get involved. But they must know what the man was getting at? The young girl seemed to know that this wasn't a normal opening question from a stranger. I looked back to the woman in the hat, she seemed ready to intervene. Good for her, someone needed to.

Before the woman could speak, the young girl muttered, "Sixteen."

"That's nice" smiled the man, but there was something hungry in his face. He looked down at her hips. "That's good," he said.

The girl looked at her feet, her hips, her hands. Anywhere but at the man. I counted half a dozen other women watching, then stared at the woman in the hat, willing her to intervene. If only she'd say something, then I could back her up.

The woman's mouth opened, and then closed as the bus stumbled to a halt again. The man got off, the teenager took a shaky breath before returning to her friends. I could only stare at the woman, enraged that she had let that happen. The woman shifted with the crowd and I could no longer see her face.

A week later, I stood in another crowd. This time in a tube station as passengers waited for the lift to the street. There was a flash of red at the front of the queue, it was the woman from the bus putting on her hat. My anger resurfaced as we filed onto the lift and rode it to ground level.

I was quite far back in the crowd, but could see the red hat ahead as we approached the ticket barriers. There was the usual shuffling of people trying to get through ahead of someone else. I saw a man wave the woman through the gates before him. He received a smile of thanks and then she was through.

The man returned the smile and followed. At the exit, the woman turned towards the bus stop. She did not see the look the man cast at her back. It was a different man from the bus, but the face held the same threat.

I walked in the same direction, towards the bus stop. My bus pulled up, and the woman boarded immediately. She took a seat behind the middle door. The man hesitated before boarding in a rush. He clearly hadn't intended to take this service, but something had changed.

I followed them onto the bus and saw the man standing in the rear doorway facing the woman. I took a seat across the aisle with a good view of them both.

As the bus moved on, the woman removed her red hat. Static caused some of her hair to fly up, and she automatically began to pat it down. She looked up and saw the man in front of her. He was nearly a metre away, but it felt too close. Her hands paused, only for a fraction. I glanced back to the man. He was staring at her intensely.

When the man knew he had the woman's full attention, he silently mouthed "You're mine".

I was shocked, did this woman know the man? Her face told me she was shocked too, and my anxiety grew. What had I stumbled into?

The man hadn't spoken out loud, and no one else on the bus would have noticed. The woman didn't know that I had seen. She turned to look out the window, hiding her face from us both. The man's smile changed. Now it felt dangerous, predatory.

We sat there for a few stops. The woman shrank, clutched her hat closer, and stared out the side window. I watched the man while he watched the woman. He seemed to grow, swell with enjoyment. I had no idea what to do.

There was nothing I could use to confront the man. His back was to the cameras, and there were no other witnesses. The only possible evidence was the interaction back at the ticket gates in front of the tube station cameras. The images would show he was polite, chivalrous even, in allowing the woman to go first. I wondered if I was overreacting. But anyone who had seen his face would know that I wasn't.

At last, the woman moved. She reached up and pushed the buzzer. I was relieved, she could escape. But now there was a new dilemma. The man was still in the doorway. She would have to pass him to exit the bus.

The man's smirk grew. The woman pressed her hat on, and clutched her jacket closer. When the bus wheezed to a stop, she stood up. Her head bowed, her whole body cringed, and she almost ran out the door.

The man looked triumphant. I was disgusted, but at least the woman was out of the situation. At the last moment, the man turned and got off the bus. The doors closed before I could move.

Outside, the woman looked back and saw the man behind her. The bus lurched on. I craned my neck to see her walking faster and the man loping behind. Why hadn't I said something?

The Red Hat recovers

"Are you OK? You look terrified?"

"Is there a man out there?"

"Out where, in the street? There are a few, why?"

"Why me, why does this happen to me?"

"What happened?"

"Is it the hat? It marks me out, but I rely on it for courage. I sound stupid, but why did I choose such a bright red one?"

"Careful, you're ripping out your hair!"

"I thought I was getting better. What did he see that made him pick me."

"You're shaking! Give me your hat and sit down. Good, now breathe. In...out... and again."

"Oh, I was so scared. That man was following me."

"Following you? Are you OK?"

"I don't, I'm not..."

"Breathe again. In...out."

"It was awful. I hope he didn't see me come in here."

"No one came in here after you."

"Are you certain?"

"Yes, that table was here before, and there's no one else."

"OK... yes. He isn't here."

"What did he look like?"

"I don't... I was trying not to look."

"Hmm."

"There really was someone..."

"It's OK, I do believe you."

"Thank you. I'm not crazy."

"No one ever thought you were."

"I did, occasionally."

"You were never crazy. You were ill, and are still recovering. But you are getting better."

“I am?”

“Yes, we see it in you. You improve every day.”

“Thank you. I needed to hear that.”

“And keep your hat. It is not the reason this happened, and you are not to blame either.”

“It keeps me warm, but I don’t fit in when wearing it.”

“No one fits in, why should you just because you’ve been ill? It’s a cheerful splash of colour, and if wearing it gives you courage, then so much the better.”

The Estate

"I don't want her not to not like me."

The woman's companions nodded in agreement, as if that mangled sentence made sense. One of the friends, the one wearing a shocking red hat, responded. "Say you need more time. You can always try later. It's never too late."

There was a chorus of agreement, and the earnest conversation continued. Liza's attention returned to that earlier, jumbled sentence. She had been following the women's conversation from her seat across the aisle, and it took Liza some effort to work through the expression.

From the earlier discussion, the woman had clearly wanted her relationship with the mysterious 'Gemma' to continue, despite 'Gemma's' unwelcome request to 'go exclusive'.

While she wasn't familiar with all the new terms these days, Liza at least knew that one. What she couldn't understand was when it had become acceptable to discuss such troubles in public, let alone this kind of relationship.

However, it seemed such openness was the trend these days. Apparently, that meant Liza should know this information, even if she didn't know the young women involved. Liza would never know if the troubled lovers could resolve their problems, as the group alighted at the next stop.

After their departure, the nearly deserted carriage provided no further distraction from her thoughts. She turned back to the window, gazing at the people on the platform without seeing them.

Liza's days were filled with a sense of disconnection recently, a feeling which the mangled language of the departed passenger seemed to reinforce. She now recognised the feeling as a barrier, an invisible wall keeping the depths of her grief hidden, even from herself. It probably wasn't healthy, but really, how did one cope with this?

Her emotional turmoil had begun three weeks previously. Liza had taken a phone call from an unknown lawyer, and heard Helen's name for the first time in years. It was only upon hearing she was an executor of the will, that Liza had learned of Helen's death.

The loss still hadn't registered when Liza spoke with her husband, later that evening. What had she said exactly? Why couldn't she remember telling John that Helen had died?

John knew of Helen, though he didn't know what Helen and Liza had really been to each other. Or did he? Sometimes Liza suspected that he did. Those rare times when John would catch his breath, as if to refrain from saying anything.

Even if he did know, did it matter? It had been years ago, when such relationships were tolerated only if they were secret. By the time the new freedoms came along, well, it was too late. The young women's conversation came back to her. You can always try later.

Liza sighed. Helen was gone, and would never answer Liza's questions now. The disappointment of today's visit was to be expected, but she had secretly hoped to find a resolution.

Not regarding the weekend in Zurich, too much time had passed for that to remain important. Once the years had healed her wounds to faded scars, there was no further desire to pick over their last few days together. Better to remember the joy and passion, than to spoil those memories with the accusations and recriminations that followed.

Today, the question Liza had wanted to be answered was why? Why did Helen keep Liza as a beneficiary in her will? This sudden shock had come into her life, upset the simple fabric of suburban living that Liza had carefully woven around her relationship with John. Was Helen reaching out from the grave to take her final revenge for the end of their affair?

That wasn't Helen's style, or at least it hadn't been when Liza had known her. But the decades weigh on everyone, and the afternoon survey of the empty cottage showed that Helen had changed over the decades.

While the lawyer and her assistants had checked cupboards or remarked on the carpet, Helen had meandered into the kitchen. The wide dining table, built for many occupants, had been worn smooth at one end. The chair there was buffed by use to a brighter colour than the others. This was where the sole inhabitant would sit and look out at the quiet lane. Liza imagined Helen sitting there day after day, watching the world go by, waiting for something to happen.

Of all the sights in the cottage, the small touches that reminded her of Helen, it was the table that shocked Liza the most. Even seeing the prized heel collection carefully packed away beneath years of dust hadn't pricked her heart as much. Helen had loved heels, and Liza never saw her in anything else, even in the bedroom. Sensible brogues with insoles were a marker of age, they were supposed to happen as life carried on.

The thought of Helen sitting among those unused chairs, the table stretching away in the empty evenings, was disturbing. It had stung Liza more than the initial news of her passing. Helen was always the centre of the party. She had been surrounded by admirers and was always generous in her affections. How did she end up alone?

Liza's reasons for leaving Helen, the betrayal and rage she felt at the time, had dulled across the years to a small, manageable sadness. A feeling she had packed away so as not to interfere with the image of a respectable councillor's wife.

Now, her troubles seemed selfish next to the realisation that Helen had lived and died alone. All of the loving and gregarious character of the past had shrunk into a small, lonely figure. One who had spent her evenings in an empty room, and had kept a lost lover in her will.

The unused chairs were Liza's undoing. Helen had meant so much to her that leaving was the only way Liza could cope. Too late did she understand that she had meant just as much to Helen.

Liza had hidden the tears for decades. Here, on a train surrounded by strangers, she could finally let them flow. This was the choice Liza had made. It was too late now. It was all too late.

The Gift

Mikale watched the new passengers press onto the train. All were too worried about missing it to let others alight first. The crush meant stragglers were still pushing on when the beeping sounded, and the doors snapped shut.

One woman with a phone in her hand shoved on at the last moment, and her coat was caught in the door. She cursed and dragged the material free before returning to her phone call. "No, not you. The door got my coat. What were you saying?"

The compartment was crowded, and the woman squeezed into a tiny gap next to Mikale's seat. Mikale shifted, turning his body away from the noise and back to his thoughts.

It was Friday evening, meaning there was only one more shopping day until his lunch with Maria and her mother on Sunday. What to buy for Mrs Lopez?

It was a delicate balancing act, something thoughtful without being too personal. It had to be the perfect gift. Not that he was sure about the perfume he had already bought for Maria. He needed to make the right impression. Perhaps...

"What? I can't believe he said that. Oh my god!"

The woman was continuing her phone call at a volume which forced him to listen. Too many people do that these days, conduct private conversations in a public place. It made him feel uncomfortable, an unwilling voyeur. Mikale glanced at the irritating woman. At least she dressed the part; her outrageous behaviour matched her scarlet hat.

Light dawned. A hat! Of course, that would have been the perfect present for Maria. She wore hats to church, so a new one would surely be welcome. It would be far more suitable than the perfume. Why had he believed the shop assistant when she had gushed, "All women love a gorgeous new scent."

The moment he'd stepped out of the store with the gaudy bag, Mikale doubted his choice. A new scent as a first gift? It was far too personal. Maria might not say as much, but her mother would. He could hear Mrs Lopez's reaction now. "What an interesting gift! A change is nice, but one can never be too careful with new things."

Mrs Lopez always looked at Mikale as if she were assessing a new carpet. Working out how best to tread all over him. Maria could enchant him with a smile, but Mrs Lopez was always there, glaring up from her wheelchair.

Maria's mother was the one blot on the bright spot of his week. Those few magic moments when he could speak to Maria and hope for her bright smile. It would start in her eyes, which brightened to a clear sparkle with teasing depths.

He was captivated the first time he saw it, who could resist? His heart sang when she smiled, and those eyes caused a rush in his stomach that he hadn't felt in years. Mikale found that he was thinking of Maria all week and looked forward to each service with renewed joy.

Every Sunday, as the congregation filed out of the church, Mikale would look for the two figures. One tall and graceful, the other hunched in a wheelchair. He would rehearse his opening lines as he crossed the churchyard. It was strange that planning for a five-minute conversation could fill hours. When he was talking to Maria, it felt like every word had unknowable weight. A test with no correct answers.

He spent his Sunday afternoons pouring over what was said, scrutinising each word or turn of her head for some hidden meaning. In those quiet hours, their conversation, which had previously held such importance, would seem normal. In fact, despite his excitement, they spoke mostly about the state of Mrs Lopez's health.

Vital minutes would tick by as he impatiently listened to the latest problem with the mother's foot or hip. While she droned on, he would feign interest and sneak glances at Maria. Once, Maria had caught him looking, and he burned with mortifying embarrassment at being caught. Whatever the new aggravation, Mrs Lopez concluded with the same complaints about "Doctors these days."

Mikale never knew whether to welcome that phrase as an end to the complaints, or to fear them as an end to the time with Maria. It was always over too soon. Mrs Lopez would wish him well and Maria would beam her wonderful smile at him. A final beacon to light his week! The warmth would linger as they picked their way across the yard, Mrs Lopez cursing the cobbles while Maria cooed her patient agreement.

But last Sunday had been different. Maria's welcoming smile was cut short. The polite greetings had faded to an awkward silence and Maria turned to gaze across the yard. The lull was broken by her mother asking after his health. It was a relief to reciprocate the question and give Mrs Lopez a chance to start the usual list of irritations. Even that had been a little stilted before Mrs Lopez had cleared her throat and glared at her daughter.

Anxious to know what was wrong, Mikale had also turned to Maria. He hoped his face had shown a polite enquiry, and not the frantic anxiety he had truly felt. Maria silently studied the ground between them. Drastic measures were called for, and it was time to apologise for his unknown trespass. As Mikale opened his mouth, Maria had burst out with, "Lunch next week?"

Mikale had gaped at her before his fears disappeared in a flood of relief. Mrs Lopez had shifted in her seat with a snort. "That is, would you be... I mean" Maria faltered, took a deep breath, and then the words rushed out. "Would you like, if you are free, perhaps you could join us for lunch next Sunday after church?"

"Yes" he had cried out, startling them all. Then "Yes, that would be most kind, I'd be delighted to accept."

The week had rushed past and now here he was, on the train with a ridiculous bottle of perfume on his knee. He didn't like the bottle and the flamboyant wrapping. They were more suited to Mrs Lopez than her daughter.

"Well, why don't you give the present to her then?"

Mikale jumped, alarmed by the sudden intrusion into his thoughts.

"Yes, I know you bought it for someone else. It sounds like they don't deserve it. Why not give the gin to her?"

The woman in the red hat had continued her phone conversation while Mikale had worried at his thoughts. It sounded like justice was being served. But it was odd how that sentence had interrupted his thoughts at just the right moment.

The perfume would be a better gift for Mrs Lopez, and might start to warm her icy gaze. Maria would probably be endeared by his gesture too.

Yes, that was perfect. Mrs Lopez would get the perfume and tomorrow he would search out a hat for Maria. The train jolted into his station and Mikale stood with a smile. He barely noticed the woman on the phone as he congratulated himself on this happy solution.

The Memory: we that are left

Third of September 2014.

The date was everywhere. Screened in bright lights on the departure board. Printed on the newspaper that lay on the train seat in front of him. Does no one else see it?, he wondered. Does no one else remember?

That morning, the radio announcer hadn't paused after reading out the date. They had just carried on with the headlines, as if the date didn't matter.

A nudge from someone brushing past caused the old man to grasp for a handhold. The transgressor, a young woman, tossed a belated "excuse me" over her shoulder. The train started to move. The man picked up the paper, and lowered himself into the seat.

Seventy-five years ago today it had started. The day Chamberlain announced the news they all feared: "this country is at war with Germany". Surely people would remember the date. It wasn't the worst day of his life. But it led directly to the one that was, as surely as death follows life.

An announcement interrupted his thoughts, and he listened carefully. The monotone voice confirmed he was on the correct train. Reassured, he felt his leg stop shaking. He was on his way and had secured a seat.

When had catching a train become such a trial? He couldn't say, but it didn't used to be so hard. He hadn't always woken early to check the route umpteen times. Maybe his granddaughter was right. Maybe ninety was too old to be travelling on his own.

Simply checking the running times is harder these days. How to work the Internet, or write a text to get departure times? You used to pick up a printed timetable and the trains ran at those times. You could set your watch by them. Now the station was full of announcements and screens covered with confusing messages. There was no one around to help any more.

He was old, of course. Hearing aids and walking sticks had replaced the bravado of his youth. But that didn't seem enough to account for all the changes. No, people have changed too. That young woman who had pushed past, for example. People used to have manners, and would wait rather than shove along. That woman wouldn't help anyone.

It wasn't just her; no one seemed to have manners any more. It was as if they were all locked in their own little world, not noticing the others around them. Not remembering what some had given. When was the last time anyone had said "thank you"? He couldn't seem to remember that either.

As he watched the woman, the train went into a tunnel. The lights flickered as the wheels screamed over the points. The woman's red hat seemed to come alive as yellow light skittered across it. The man's breath caught and his pulse quickened. The screaming of the metal grew unbearable, and so like those twisted engines. Blackness encroached, and he was lost to that hectic night once more.

It was supposed to be a routine flight. A night raid on a suspected bomb factory in northern Germany. Straight flights, keep in formation, deliver the payload and back in time for bacon & eggs. Until that cold February night.

The target was sighted and the bomb dropped. Not a direct hit, but effective enough. Evans had been improving in the last couple of raids. The captain ordered the run home and had just promised another round in the airfield bar.

A massive impact came with no warning. The plane was smashed sideways, and he was thrown against the fuselage. There was a terrible screech of metal, the engines roared and sputtered. The plane started to spin downwards, always down.

He was shouting into the radio, god knows what he was saying. Whatever had been drilled into him during training. The floor flew up to meet him, and his world exploded into darkness.

Coming up out of the void, he heard a roar of flames and the pinging of hot metal. Someone was shouting and someone else screaming. There was something on his temple, and a stabbing pain which nearly knocked him out again. The terrible screams stopped, and he could hear now that the shouts were edged with terror. Slowly, unwillingly, he formed the noise into words. They were shouting his name. He forced his eyes to open.

The world was still black, but edged with flickering light. High above him, shadows swirled against the stars. There were brief flares of explosions. The shouts stopped, and the view above was blocked by a familiar face. "Thank god you're awake. The captain is bad, but Bexley and Hunter didn't make it. We thought you wouldn't either, but you must have a thick skull under there."

Evans thrust a canteen into his hand and disappeared. After a sip, he lay back. The last he remembered was hitting his head. He felt gingerly around the throbbing pain. There was a bandage, which didn't seem to be doing much to stop the blood. His blood.

He took a deep breath and sat up. The world swam, but he gritted his teeth and waited for it to settle. He had been pulled free from the blazing hulk of metal which used to be the plane. Over to the right, where the screams had come from, were two disturbing shapes. He caught his breath as the world threatened to go black again.

Bexley and Hunter didn't make it.

He couldn't think of that now. Needed to keep himself together. We were on a mission. We got the target. Bexley and Hunter didn't make it.

We were headed home. We were shot down. Bexley and Hunter didn't make it.

We were still over Germany. Bexley and Hunter didn't make it.

We are still in Germany. Bexley and Hunter didn't make it.

We are still in Germany.

We have to move.

I have to move.

I have to get up.

Now!

The old man jerked to his feet and lost his balance. Disorientated from the vivid memory, he realised he was in a train carriage, but couldn't remember why. He was leaning against a young woman who had caught his fall. She was looking at him, asking if he was OK.

"Yes" he croaked. Then he cleared his throat and assured the woman that he was fine. They sat down again. The woman offered him some water, which he gratefully accepted. The old man recovered his breath and composure while the train rumbled on. The woman returned to her book, losing herself into the story.

Bexley wouldn't have sat here watching her. He'd have been straight over. Never lost a chance to talk to the ladies, did Bexley. With so many on the go, he'd never managed to keep a lady either. Hunter and Evans teased him about that. Well, teased and admired him for it. Bexley would grin back. "It's a gift lads, what can I say?"

The woman smiled as she read something amusing. I was wrong about you, he thought. The lads would like you, too. You'd probably like them, you'd like their jokes. Well, maybe not Hunter's jokes. No one liked those.

But the lads are all gone now. You won't know them, or what they did. I wish you knew them. I'd like to tell you about them.

The train jostled into a station and the young woman stood. She nodded at him, then turned and left the train. Her red hat bobbed past the window and was gone. The old man sighed: "They shall not grow old".

The Rush

Joan looked into the hallway mirror and patted a wayward grey hair into place. Her mother had always sent her out the door with the reminder that to do her best, she needed to look her best. This had installed a life-long habit, and today Joan felt the need for her departed mother's reassurance.

It had been months since that embarrassing slip on the ice, which had kept her housebound for weeks. Yet, Joan still felt a change in herself. While the painful wrist sprain and colourful bruising were nicely healed, small niggles remained.

The weeks spent inside during the dark days of winter had been soothing at first, a cocoon protecting her from the world. Later, they had become a trap which slowed more than just her body. She found that simple conversations were difficult. Her brain was becoming stiff and slow alongside her body. That was what today was about, a first step to feeling normal again.

Joan stood with keys in hand and went through her morning errands: first up the hill to the post office, then across to collect the prescription. Her daughter, Carol, had suggested this outing. Or rather, had commanded it.

"You need to start moving again. This isn't like you. Spring is coming. It's warming up, and you can't sit inside all day. What you need is a short and familiar walk to build up confidence again."

Joan had scoffed at this, she was safe in her little house. But, deep down, she knew her daughter was right. Not that Joan would admit it. Another of her mother's daily lessons came back to her: the hardest part of life is admitting you were wrong.

Joan sighed, she couldn't put this off any longer. It was time to move. A final check confirmed that the letter was in her handbag, then Joan stepped out into a cool spring morning. The remnants of a late frost lingered in the air, but the sun high in a clear blue sky promised warmth.

The bright daffodils lining her path lent Joan their cheer as she walked to the front gate. She stepped onto the pavement, then turned to admire the flowers again. They were looking better than ever this year. Carol's tip, to cut them back later in the summer, had proven its worth.

A high-pitched squeal cut into Joan's thought, as another voice cried, "look out!" Something thumped into her side and Joan careened into the garden wall. Her shoes lost their footing, and her arms flailed as fear took over. "No, I mustn't fall!" she cried out.

A strong hand caught Joan's arm. "Woah, careful now. Got you" said a reassuring female voice.

Shaking, Joan grasped at this support. The friendly stranger helped her to rest against the wall. Her pulse was racing and she took short, ragged breaths. "Oh my. Oh my." Joan gasped, keeping her head down until the shock settled.

Her view of the pavement was blocked by a concerned face surrounded by a red halo. After a moment of confusion, Joan realised the halo was the brim of a hat. "Are you OK?" the newcomer asked. "That was a nasty bump."

"What happened?" Joan looked at her rescuer, a younger woman with a red hat squished onto unkempt hair. Beyond, further along the pavement, Joan saw a girl wobbling on a scooter and looking back at them. When the girl saw Joan looking, she scowled, then turned away and pushed off. The scooter built up speed as the child rode down the hill.

The woman next to Joan spoke again. "That child bounced off you before she stopped. Are you OK, are you hurt?"

Joan took a deep breath and silently asked herself the same question. Her pulse slowed, and she noticed other sensations. Her hip throbbed. A dull ache, not the bright pain that indicated a bad injury. There was a softer throb in her arm where the woman's grasp had righted her, and the back of her hand stung with a graze from the wall.

"I'm OK, I think. Rather shaken." Joan managed.

"I'm not surprised, that was quite some momentum the girl had built up. Lucky it wasn't a direct hit, really."

Joan let out a heavy sigh. "Are you sure you're OK?" The woman repeated, "Can I help you call someone...?"

"No, I'm fine. Thank you for your help. I'll just catch my breath for a moment."

"OK, well..." The woman was interrupted by a loud shout from nearby.

"Tamsin, stop at the corner, honey." They turned together to see another woman approaching. The new arrival was pushing a pram and looking past them to the girl on the scooter.

"Ah, the mother finally arrives," the woman muttered, and glanced back at Joan.

Oh dear, thought Joan. I'm not ready for this. I know something must be said, I just can't right now. Her reluctance must have shown as the woman gave a nod. "Take it easy for a wee while," she said.

"Yes, thank you again." Joan smiled.

"You're very welcome." Then the woman turned, adjusted her hat and intercepted the mother. "Excuse me, but your child was going very fast and knocked over this elderly lady."

Joan was dismayed. Elderly lady? It had been a rough couple of months but, elderly? The mother was surprised too, and halted next to them. "What?"

"It could have been really nasty." The woman in the red hat continued. "You should really slow her down."

Joan was relieved that the point had been made. The stranger had helped her a second time this morning. All Joan needed to do was accept the mother's apology with grace. "How dare you tell me what to do?" The mother's voice rose.

"Your child nearly caused a serious injury. I'm just saying, it's lucky no one was badly hurt."

The mother gaped while the rescuer cast a quick nod at Joan, then continued her journey up the hill. The mother stared at Joan, who watched the woman's face turn from indignation to anger.

No apology from her, thought Joan. As the mother opened her mouth, Joan braced herself. But after a short hesitation, the mother spun around and shouted after the departing woman: "Look, my parenting is fine, thanks! I don't need your stupid advice, and nor do my kids."

When there was no reply, the mother added, "And get a new hat, you rude woman. Think you can go around telling people what to do!"

The lady with the red hat continued up the hill, showing no sign of turning, nor even that she heard. The mother turned to Joan. "Honestly, some people, happy to tell others what to do but won't listen themselves. Like, my girl didn't hit you. Did she?"

"Well, yes she did."

"Oh." There was a pause. "But you weren't knocked over or anything."

"Actually, yes. I..."

The mother interrupted: "Onto the ground, I mean."

"Well, I wasn't knocked to the ground, no. But..."

"See, I knew she was lying. Horrible woman, lying and trying to get my kids in trouble."

Joan was not sure what to say. The mother continued. "It's those that don't have kids themselves that lash out at those that do. You have kids?"

Joan was uncertain why her Carol was involved, but cautiously murmured assent.

"See, so you know how it is. Kids will be kids. It's not their fault they're running around. It's what kid's do, and it's just mean to tell them off. A child can't be expected to have rules and responsibilities."

Joan knew who had responsibility, but didn't feel ready to face the sort of abuse dished out to her now-absent helper. However, an apology was called for, so she rallied herself.

"But, still…" she did not get the chance to finish as the mother suddenly screeched: "Tamsin stop! I told you to wait at the corner."

The mother grabbed the pram and broke into a panicked run. Looking down the hill, Joan watched the child stop in the road, then sulkily retreat to the pavement and her mother's scolding. "Why can't you stop? Why can't you see it isn't safe? I told you not to do that. Why can't you remember the rules?"

Joan leaned on the wall and steadied herself for a moment longer. She debated whether to go back indoors and have a cup of tea. But Carol was right, she did need to move. Joan turned up the hill, already rehearsing the story of her first outing for Carol. She hadn't thought to thank the kind stranger who helped her, which was a shame.

Joan realised she could thank someone else, and added another errand to her mental list. A stop at the florist for Carol's favourite flowers. But what to say on the card? Her mother's voice rang in her head again: Always thank those who point out your errors, they are the ones who truly care for you.

The Found

Gary saw the mismatched pair as he swung his response car into the side street. An elderly man crumpled at one end of a bench near the entrance to a park. At the other end of the bench was a middle-aged woman wearing a bright red hat. That fitted the description given over the call.

Sure enough, the woman signalled for his attention, then relaxed when he acknowledged. Gary took this as a good sign. This hadn't sounded like a difficult call, but he'd learned to be on guard. He pulled over close to the park gate, and called out, "I won't be a moment, just getting my gear."

As the woman waved again, Gary heard her reassure the man. "See, I told you we'd sort this out."

The old man mumbled a bit through his unkempt beard, and smiled at her. Gary hefted his gear and made his way through the gate. The woman spoke first, relief in her face & voice. "Thank you so much for coming, I wasn't sure what to do next".

"That's what we're here for." Gary smiled as he turned to her companion. "Why don't you tell me what's happened so far."

The man's face changed. "Home, I'm going home. It's not far, I know. But..." His voice faltered, he looked down at his clenched fists. "I know it's not far. My memory. Bad."

Gary sighed, and glanced at the woman. She was still watching the man. Her face was kind, but there was something else there. Fear. He wondered what was scary about this frail man.

The woman turned and saw Gary looking at her. "I found him by the bus stop. Well, really, I saw him there three or four hours ago but didn't think anything of it. When I was going out again just now, I realised he was still there. He was shuffling up and down, looking lost. So, I asked if he needed help."

She paused and tilted her head at Gary; silently asking the question: was that right? Did I do the right thing?

He knew why she, why everyone, questioned their Good Samaritan acts. Acting out of the norm, despite good intentions, brings guilt. Well, Gary couldn't absolve her. Might not even be able to help her. This job gets harder every day. But he couldn't say that to a stranger. In the end, Gary just nodded. "Go on".

"Well, he just said that. Just said 'Memory bad', and I felt I had to help him." Her hand found the old man's arm and patted it gently. "He said he was trying to get home, but got this far and no further. He must have been walking up and down in the same spot for hours."

The woman shuddered, and Gary knew then that it wasn't the man which she feared. After a pause, she continued. "Anyway, he couldn't tell me his name or where he lived. Could only keep saying that his memory is bad."

"Yes" the man's reedy voice piped up. "I'm going home. But memory, bad."

He started to wring his hands and rock back and forth on the bench. Gary took a step back and thought: whoa, need to calm him. The woman acted before he did. "Hey, don't worry. We'll help you out. Take some more water."

She gently pushed a water bottle into the man's hands, which stopped the compulsive movements and brought a small smile to his face. The man calmed a little, and Gary asked, "What's your name, mate?"

Wrong question, the smile slid away and the man's head shook from side to side. "Memory, bad. Don't know."

"It's Jack." They both turned to the woman.

The old man mouthed the name slowly, "Jack. Jack... yes". His smile returned and he sat back happily.

At Gary's silent inquiry, the woman explained. "Jack has a hospital band on his wrist. That's why I thought I'd better call emergency services. But first, we came to the park for somewhere quiet away from the main road. And I gave him water. I didn't know how long it's been since his last drink and, well..."

She trailed off and they both contemplated the drool caking Jack's beard and thin t-shirt. Some fresh, some obviously hours old. That decided things for Gary.

"Right then. Jack, I'd like you to put this blanket on while I take your temperature."

Jack recoiled immediately, "No. No blankets. I'm not..."

The pain on Jack's face stung Gary. Damn it, he thought. I was wrong, this is a hard job.

The woman rescued them again by taking the blanket from Gary's hand and unfolding it. "It's such a lovely bright red, Jack. See, it matches my hat!"

Jack stared at the woman, shocked out of his pain. "I bet it would look good on you, Jack. Shall we try it on?" At Jack's uncertain nod, she wound the blanket over his shoulders. "Yep, it definitely suits you."

Jack grinned and hugged the blanket to his throat, inspecting it carefully. Gary mouthed a silent thanks to the woman and popped the thermometer into Jack's ear.

The three of them sat quietly for a minute. Around them, the park was beautiful in the early evening. Raucous children carried on with their games, oblivious to the drama in their midst. Their squealing caught Jack's attention. His face brightened, and the sudden joy was infectious even under the hedge of unkempt beard.

Gary smiled at Jack encouragingly, "Kids, just their laughter cheers you up."

Jack nodded, looking at Gary properly for the first time. "I had children once, have grandchildren now. They enjoy playing too." Jack frowned. "At least. I think they do."

Gary winced as Jack's bewilderment returned. A small beep told Gary that Jack's temperature was fine. He pulled the thermometer away as loud giggling caught Jack's attention.

By the time Gary had packed his bag up, Jack was grinning at the children. Not wanting to disturb him, Gary moved round to the woman. "He seems fine. I suspect he's absconded this morning, but I need to call it in."

"Absconded?"

Her shock was clear, so Gary corrected himself quickly. "I mean, I think Jack was admitted to hospital but left because the ward wasn't familiar."

"Does that happen often, people just walking out with no-one noticing?"

"Unfortunately, yes. We often get called out to deal with confused patients who don't understand why they were in hospital. They just don't have the staff to look after everyone. All the money goes on bombs, not sick people."

The last sentence was out before Gary could stop it, and he reprimanded himself for the lack of professionalism. Gary hadn't meant to be so cynical, but this call had got to him. They seemed to get to most folks in this job if you hung around too long. Not that many people did hang around these days. Why deal with the low pay when Australia would welcome you with open arms, and wallets?

Sighing, Gary turned away to use his radio. The woman nodded thoughtfully to herself and wrapped the blanket closer around Jack's shoulders. Jack would soon be back in his safe, controlled environment. For now, he watched the children play, oblivious to his recent despair.

The woman quietly gathered her belongings and stood to go. "Bye Jack, you take care now."

Jack looked at her, then up at her hat. "Red. Red suits me too. Someone told me that once, can't remember who. My memory, bad."

The Red Hat retained

"So you are telling me that after all your trauma, you were actually helping a strange man? That is why you cancelled last week."

"Yes, I'm sorry. I didn't feel I could leave him."

"No need to apologise. That was a lovely thing you did."

"I just saw his face...the fear and loneliness. I've spent months feeling that way. When I recognised those feelings, I simply couldn't walk past."

"It is an extraordinary thing."

"Surely not, surely other people would have stepped in to help him?"

"Well, maybe. But they obviously hadn't as he was there for hours before you helped. So, perhaps not?"

"Oh, you think I was wrong to help?"

"No, you were right to help. I also think it took extraordinary courage given all that you've been through."

"When you put it that way. Yes, I do feel more confident."

"It is good progress."

"Thank you, I do still second guess myself."

"Everyone does. Your illness means you think it's all connected. Whereas second guessing is just normal behaviour."

"True, I did that before all this. It's been a rough six months."

"Yes, and now it's a lovely spring day. I was going to suggest a walk now that we've finished the coffee."

"That sounds lovely, let's do it."

"Don't forget your red hat, it's fallen off the table."

"Whoops. It is getting a bit warm for the hat now. Time to put it away, though I suppose the chill will come again."

"Yes, but now you are ready for it."

Epilogue

The woman sitting in the café's window waved out at one of the pedestrians waiting to cross at the traffic lights. Her friend waved back, then mimed taking a large bite. The woman in the café giggled, and gave a thumbs up in return.

The woman rose and made for the counter, but did not get far before returning. She pulled a red hat from her bag and placed it prominently in the middle of the table. Satisfied that the seats were marked as taken, she walked up to the counter. "You can order through the app now," said the barista.

"Yes, thank you. But my friend would like a Pastéis de Nata and you only have one left..."

An older lady popped her head out of the café's small kitchen, and greeted the woman. "Hullo there, I thought you two would be in again today."

"Hi Lisa. Yep, Thursday coffee can't be missed."

"Who would set the world to rights, if not you two?"

"Exactly!"

Lisa turned to the young server. "These ladies will have a chocolate brownie, the last Pastéis de Nata, and two flat whites."

"Oh dear, you know us too well."

"I've picked a few things up over the years. Enjoy your catch-up."

The woman was just paying as her friend walked in the door. "Thank you, my treat next time." The newcomer hugged the first woman, then picked up the two plates. "Shall I take these?"

"I'll follow with the coffees. We're in the..."

"Yes, in the window seat. I saw your hat."

The two friends settled and began an animated conversation. Once the week's updates and anecdotes had been exchanged, the newcomer cleared her throat. "It has been a while since I saw that hat. Is everything...OK?"

"Oh, yes. The anniversary is coming up, and I have been reminiscing a bit."

"I thought it was about this time of year that your injury occurred."

"Yes, it was. But it took ages to work out what was happening after that blow to the head."

"Until they found out how much...damage had occurred?"

"Mmm, those were difficult days. No one knew what was going on. Ten years can feel like such a long time and no time at all."

"Oh gosh, yes. It has been a full decade, it was just before I moved here."

"Which also means that we've been coming to Lisa's Café for ten years."

"Well, you don't get tarts like this just anywhere, you know."

"Do you mean me, or..."

They both giggled and shared the last piece of pastry.

"So, it is reminiscing which has brought the hat out? No relapses?"

"Oh, is that what you are worried about? No, nothing like that." The woman picked up her red hat. "I was just thinking about those days. Ten years is a big anniversary and much has changed. I had a different life before the injury."

"Do you miss it?"

"Sometimes. I had more friends back then, only a precious few hung around during the long recovery. I guess I wasn't that fun to be with."

"No, but a good friend would stay."

They grinned at each other. The woman looked down at her hat and said, "Yeah, that was a hard lesson to learn. But I got so much help from those who stayed." She paused, "and from strangers too."

"Strangers?"

"Some of the clearest memories from that time are of strangers. You know, small interactions when you are just out and about, on the tube, or elsewhere."

"Why would you remember them?"

"I think...Sometimes I think it is our actions towards strangers which show us who we really are. And sometimes, well, I didn't like who I saw."

"So you did better. You saw someone you didn't like and changed."

"True. Plus, no one is the same person they were ten years ago."

"Yes. Look at you now — a gallery opening!"

"Oh, yes. I need to be there soon. Want to come early and 'quality test' the bubbly?"

"Sounds like an important job. Let's go then."

The two were chatting loudly as they left the café. Later that evening, the cleaner found the red hat where it had fallen between the cushions.

Thank you for reading *The Red Hat Stories*.

You can sign up for more on from the author at:

www.pigpen.page/newsletter

Acknowledgements

I dedicate this book with gratitude to Christine, my writing teacher, who nagged me for years to finish the stories.

There are several others who helped to ensure this book is as good as it could be. My thanks to:

Jen, for her continued critique, constructive feedback, and our shared writing sessions;

Soheb Mahmoud, Rita Beaumont, Ian H., and C.F., who gave their time and enthusiasm as beta readers;

K. Powell, for putting up with my whinging, and providing a superb cover;

Hilary, for my well-thumbed copy of *Dreyer's English*;

And my family and friends for their support and encouragement.

Kickstarter backers

This paperback was initially published with the awesome support of:

- A. Thomas,
- Alexander Davies,
- Chloe Ormerod,
- Claire Stening,
- Dad :),
- David and Rebekah Kelly
- David Edwards,
- Elizabeth Kelly,
- Emma and Florence Barham,
- Evelin, Polly's number 1 supporter,
- Gill Gillies,
- Hilary & Paul,
- Hugh,
- Ivan Sanchez,
- Ian Hunter
- Jennifer Flippance,
- Jeremy Wilkinson,
- Joanna Deeprose-Dent,
- John Rae,
- Judy O'Connor, (Mum)
- Minz,
- Patricia Broad,
- Paul Redfern,
- Orna Ross,
- Richard Novak,
- Rory C.,
- Siobhán Boyle DW,
- Soheb Mahmood,
- Susan Hunter,
- Theresa Robinson,
- Tiest Vilee,
- and Zedstar!